AF441680

# LIFE STORY OF TOMIOKA GIYU [THE WATER HASHIRA]

DIPAYAN MITRA

Copyright © Dipayan Mitra
All Rights Reserved.

This book has been published with all efforts taken to make the material error-free after the consent of the author. However, the author and the publisher do not assume and hereby disclaim any liability to any party for any loss, damage, or disruption caused by errors or omissions, whether such errors or omissions result from negligence, accident, or any other cause.

While every effort has been made to avoid any mistake or omission, this publication is being sold on the condition and understanding that neither the author nor the publishers or printers would be liable in any manner to any person by reason of any mistake or omission in this publication or for any action taken or omitted to be taken or advice rendered or accepted on the basis of this work. For any defect in printing or binding the publishers will be liable only to replace the defective copy by another copy of this work then available.

# Contents

# Prologue

This story is about Demon Slayers from the Japanese manga Kimetsu No Yaiba.

As many people don't like to watch anime and also doesn't know where to watch them, they can buy this book and learn about them.

My contact info is given below:

Gmail: mitradipayan03@gmail.com.

Twitter: @SNIPERDMYT47.

If you like this book then please consider refer this book to your friends and families.

# CHAPTER ONE

# EARLY LIFE

Giyu grew up alongside his older sister Tsutaku. When he was still a child, her sister sacrificed herself to protect him from the demons. After the death of Tsutaku Giyu tried to tell others that a demon had killed his sister. However, he was labeled as mentally unstable and was sent away to one of his relatives, who was a doctor at that time. Giyu eventually ran away during the journey there and almost died on a mountain due to the harsh climate & cold.

He was later rescued and became apprenticed under Sakonji Urokodaki. Giyu was only 13 years old when he met while training under Sakonji, where they eventually became good friends due to their age and nearly similar past. Together they entered the final selection on Mount Fuji Kasani. Unfortunately, Giyu was injured after a demon's attack and was saved by Sabito, who nearly defeated every demon on the mountain. However, after the week went by, it was revealed to Giyu that Sabito was the only one who died on the final selection exams.

As a result, Giyu started developing doubts about the authenticity of his position after becoming the Water Hashira as he ought to Destroy ALL the evil DEMONS.

Giyu's ought to Destroy ALL the evil DEMONS.

# CHAPTER TWO

# FINAL SELECTION ARC

While Tanjiro was struggling to fend off the attack from his demon-turned-sister Nezuko, Giyu attacked the latter from behind, only to fail as Tanjiro moved Nezuko out of the way. After recovering quickly, Giyu asked the boy why he protected the demon. To which he replied that the demon was his sister. He was looking at the maddened Nezuko Giyu, questioning this statement before swiftly removing the girl from her brother's grip.

Giyu attacking demon turned Nezuko from behind.

Tanjiro begs Giyu to spare the life of Nezuko, but Giyu becomes angry and states that he has no authority over who lives/dies. He continues by saying that Tanjiro is too weak to protect his family & all of his talk about finding his sister's condition and fighting his family's killer is ridiculous. Giyu also states that he could've skewered them both and done with it. As the boy ponders it, Giyu silently encourages him to find the result necessary to accomplish all of the lofty goals he had played upon himself.

Giyu swiftly removes Nezuko from Tanjiro's grip.

He then stabs Nezuko in the chest causing Tanjiro to throw a stone at him in a fury. Giyu blocks the stone with the hilt of his sword & avoiding the objectives as Tanjiro charges at him. Seeing the attack attempt is only a simple act of emotion. Giyu angrily drives the sword's hilt into Tanjiro's back, causing him to knock out, staring at the fallen Tanjiro where his opponent's axe is. Looking up, he sees the weapon charging at him at full speed, but he manages to dodge the axe by tilting his head to the right.

Giyu angrily drives the swords hilt in the back of Tanjiro's back causing him to knock out.

He then acknowledged Tanjiro's strategy that he came empty-handed, and knowing that he couldn't win against Giyu, he made a distraction. While distracted, Nezuko kicks Giyu with extreme strength because she has become a demon and dodged back in an attacking position. He immediately curses himself and sees that she is going towards the unconscious Tanjiro to devour him [or so he thought]. To his surprise, Nezuko angrily defends him & suddenly charges toward Giyu to attack him. Giyu then sheathes his sword and incapacitates the unusual demon, Nezuko, with a bare-handed blow to the neck.

Giyu strikes Nezuko making her unconscious.

While Tanjiro is unconscious, Giyu wraps the unconscious Nezuko in a clean cloth and a bamboo muzzle-like tube in her mouth. When Tanjiro regains consciousness, Giyu instructs him to visit Sakonji Urokodaki in the mountains and suggests Tanjiro not take Nezuko out in the Sun.

He later sent a letter to Sakonji Urokodaki requesting him to train Tanjiro while explaining the conditions he's making this request.

Giyu tells Tanjiro to meet Sakonji Urokodaki.

# CHAPTER THREE

# MOUNT NATAGUMO ARC

After receiving news of the mini Mizunoto Ranks & Lower Rank Demon Slayers being dead / killed by Demons on Mount Natagumo. Giyu went to take a look at the situation along with Kochou Shinobu [The Insect Hashira] to assist the lower-rank swordsman. Upon his arrival, Giyu saves Inosuke from the father-spider demon by cutting off its arm and easily beheading the demon in a single strike. Inosuke quickly becomes a fan of his technique and demands him to a duel. Giyu tells him to go back to training & also that he wasn't strong enough to fight any Demon / Hashiras. Giyu ties Inosuke up on a tree with a rope while Inosuke screams to fight with him.

Giyu later intervenes by getting into the battle of Tanjiro and Lower Moon 5 Rui. He saves Tanjiro from Rui's Blood Demon Art. He also praises Tanjiro for holding out so long against the 11th Strongest Demon, specially selected by Kibutsuji Muzan. Rui then gets frustrated and attempts to use his blood demon art, "Cutting Thread Rotation." But suddenly, Giyu nullifies the attack and saves Tanjiro once again. He then proceeded to decapitate Rui in a single slash showing his strength as an Hashira.

Giyu ties up Inosuke on a tree.

Then he says that Shinobu suddenly appeared and was trying to attach Nezuko. Giyu deflects her attack and gracefully lands. Then she tells Giyu to move aside as she wants to kill the Demon girl Nezuko. Giyu didn't reply and asked Tanjiro if he could move. He then picks up Nezuko and starts to run by continuously thanking him and apologizing to him simultaneously. After the 2 Hashiras are alone, Shinobu warns Giyu not to interfere as he's violating the Demon Slayer Code of Conduct rules.

BUT TOMIOKA-SAN, THIS IS A VIOLATION OF HUNTERS CONDUCT.
. . . . .
WHAT DO YOU INTEND ON DOING?
YOU'RE OBSTRUCTING THE DEMON KILLING.

Giyu holds Shinobu under his arms to prevent her from chasing Tanjiro and Nezuko.

After the siblings escape, Giyu manages to hold Shinbu under his arm and prevent her from chasing after them. But a Kasugai Crow (The crows used by the Demon Slayer Corpse to communicate with the Hashiras and the Demon Slayers all across the country) interrupts and tells Shinobu Kochou to bring Tanjiro and Nezuko to the HQ (Head Quarters).

# CHAPTER FOUR

# REHABILITATION ARC

Giyu and the other Hashiras gathered at the HQ, where Giyu stood alone from others as he Violated the rules where Tanjiro and Nezuko were on trial. Kagaya Ubuyashiki (The Current Leader of the Demon Slayer) arrived, and the Hahsiras bowed in respect.

Kagaya appears with his 2 daughters

Here he brings out a letter sent to him by a Former Water Hashira named Sakonji Urokodaki. He was also the trainer of the present Water Hashira Tomioka Giyu and Tanjiro Kamado. He also took care of Nezuko while Tanjiro was out for his training in the mountains. In the letter, he stated that He and Giyu would commit Seppuku if Nezuko ever craved human blood / killed any human from hunger. After hearing Giyu's and Urokodaki's sacrifice to keep them alive Tanjiro breaks into tears and thanks them for believing him and his sister.

Giyu & Urokodaki will commit Seppuku if Nezuko ever craved human blood / killed any human from hunger.

He also angrily stated that He would surely bring Muzan to his death and would not spare him for what he had done for the past 1,000 years. Later he was carried by the workers to the Butterfly Mansion, where he reunited with Zenitsu and Inosuke after fighting the Spider Demon family. There the 3 of them trained, took medicines & concentrated on their breathing techniques to fight the demons more effectively.

Zenitsu - Thunder Breathing. (Although he could only learn the 1ˢᵗ form, he created his own four extensions so that he could fight).

Inosuke - Beast Breathing. (This breathing style is created by Inosuke while living in the mountains).

Tanjiro - Water & Hinokami Kagura (The Water Breathing is the most common type of breathing taught in the Demon Slayer Corps, whereas THE HINOKAMI KAGURA can only be passed down to exceptionally Kamado family for generations) Later, it was revealed that it was THE MOST POWERFUL BREATHING STYLE & THE FIRST BREATHING STYLE CREATED BY YORIICHI TSUGIKUNI.

# CHAPTER FIVE

# HASHIRA TRAINING ARC

Following the Swordsmith Village Arc events, Giyu attends an Emergency Meeting with the other Hasiras, where they discuss the Demon Slayer Marks. Oyakata says that this mark can only be obtained with this Hashira Training. Giyu suddenly decides to leave. He was annoyed, but then Shinobu requested Giyu to explain his reason for leaving the meeting. Giyu says that he is different from the other Hasiras and leaves.

After Tanjiro gets healed from the fight with Upper Moon 6 siblings (Daki & Gyutaro), he receives a letter from Kagaya to talk one-on-one with Giyu and convince him to work alongside the other Hasiras. Tanjiro accepted the letter and later visited Giyu and spoke about the Hashira Training. After Tanjiro asks Giyu why he is mad, he tells Tanjiro that he should've stuck to The Water Breathing and become the Water Hashira as he is not worthy of holding the position. Tanjiro kept on asking questions as to what he meant by the words.

Tanjiro visits Giyu's house

Then suddenly, Giyu admitted that he never really did pass the Final Selection Arc. Giyu reveals that he was in the same team as Sabito & also that he befriended him as under the instruction of Sakonji Urokodaki. He also told him how Sabito saved him and went on to defeat nearly every Demon all by himself, and on the mountain, before his unfortunate death, Giyu had never really defeated any Demons. However, he still passed the Final Selection Arc, which made him unsuitable for the position of Hashira. He also said that if Sabito had not died, he would have awakened his Demon Slayer Mark much earlier.

After hearing this story of Giyu, Tanjiro relates the story to his life story as he had to watch Rengoku (The Flame Hasira) die in front of him and that he could not do anything to stop Azaka (Upper Moon 3) from killing him. He also recalled how He, Zenitsu & Inosuke survived the fierce fight because Rengoku was a Hashira and much stronger than the 3 Demon Slayers combined.

After hearing o the painful story of Giyu, Tanjiro asks him if he has fulfilled Sabito's wish. Giyu was shocked as he suddenly recalled what Sabito had said to him during the training and was also reminded of the same by Urokodaki-san. He then remembered that Sabito told him not to die and let his sister's death go in vain. Giyu then convinces himself, apologizes to his subordinates, and promises Tanjiro that he will participate in the Hashira Training Arc.

After completing the training, Tanjiro visited Giyu, and he saw a massive spar going on between Giyu and Sanemi (The Wind Hashira). He sees that both of them are fighting intensely with wooden swords. After some time, Giyu's sword breaks, and Sanemi proposes a fistfight. Tanjiro interrupts them and asks Sami to calm down. He also offers to eat Rice Dumplings together as he thinks he would be happy. Suddenly Sanemi punches Tanjiro causing him to knock out and storm off in anger. Tanjiro wakes up a few moments later and asks Giyu what has happened between them. Giyu explains that he and Sanemi were not fighting but were training. He further explains that as Hashiras are much stronger than any normal Demon Slayers, they need to train with other Hashiras to maintain a high level of strength.

After which, Tanjiro and Giyu became like friends & Sanemi was also pleased to see them together.

# CHAPTER SIX

# INFINITY CASTLE ARC

After Ubuyashiki & his families die while trying to kill Muzan, Giyu, along with the other Hashira, come running to see the matter of the explosion and find Muzan struggling to regenerate Hashiras do not waste a single second and start attacking Muzan.

Tanjiro comes face to face with Akaza Again.

To Giyu's surprise, he, along with all the other Hashiras, teleported to Muzan's Infinity Castle, where he could control everything because of the Blood Demon Arts of Upper Moon 4 Nakime (also known as the Biwa Demon). While confused, they both suddenly encounter Upper Moon 3 Akaza. By seeing him, Tanjiro went furious and started attacking him without thought. Tanjiro also screams his name and says he was never the winner in the fight between Akaza & Rangoku (The Flame Hashira).

However, Akaza has already launched his punches at Tanjiro. Afterward, Tanjiro could narrowly escape his punches using his Hinokami Kagura technique. After witnessing this small fight, Giyu was amazed by Tanjro's techniques & that it matches the level of a Hashira.

Tanjiro screams out Akaza's name in anger.

However, Akaza has already launched his punches at Tanjiro. Afterward, Tanjiro could narrowly escape his punches using his Hinokami Kagura technique. After witnessing this small fight, Giyu was amazed by Tanjro's techniques & that it matches the level of a Hashira.

He then recalls the snowy day when he first met Tanjiro & how all he could do was beg for his sister Nezuko's life. Compared to how he fights without fearing losing his life or dignity, Giyuu unleashes his Water Breathing technique to maneuver around Akaza.

After noticing this, Akaza said, "It has been 50 years since I last fought against a Water Hashira. After that, Akaza unleashed his Destructive Death technique, which he previously used against Rengoku.

Giyu attacks Akaza to save Tanjiro.

Giyu swifts backward with water dance and slices Azaka's right hand, but he quickly regenerates and attacks Tanjiro. By seeing this, Tanjiro was shocked but tried to dodge the attack. The speed of Akaza's blow was so much that Giyu saved him, but Tanjiro slammed against the Infinity castle's walls due to its force.

However, Akaza tries to attack Tanjiro's neck after regenerating, and due to Tanjiro's physical condition, he cannot dodge quickly and is saved by Giyu. Giyu then realized that Akaza's generation was happening faster than average, which confused him. He quickly calculated that when Akaza was fighting, he was using some Blood Demon Arts that helped him regenerate faster than his average speed. Seeing this, Giyu warns Tanjiro about him, but Akaza is ready to punch Giyu through walls and even buildings before he can react.

Akaza then throws Giyu with his super strength, and Tanjiro tries to talk with Akaza but then disrespects Rengoku (The Flame Hashira) in front of Tanjiro to piss him off. Tanjiro almost fell for the trick, but he suddenly recovered and asked Akaza if he remembered something from when he was a Human.

Tanjiro asks Akaza if he remembers something from his past.

This angered Akaza, and he kicked Tanjiro so hard that he broke through 4 walls and became unconscious. After witnessing this, Giyu was furious and came at an extreme speed to attack Akaza, which confused him for a moment. Giyu then saw that Akaza had boosted his physical strength further, and now he was in his peak physical capabilities in his demon form.

Giyu had never faced someone with this extreme physical form, and he started thinking that it was no joke that Rengoku lost the battle with him and also how strong Rengoku was to hold onto Akaza until the Sunrise. He then understands that this battle would be of life and death and that he could die in this fight with Akaza as this was an actual test of one's capabilities. To Tanjiro's and Akaza's surprise, Giyu unlocked his Demon Slayer Mark. Giyu then rushed forward and struck Akazas neck, but Akaza dodged the attack and then praised Giyu for going beyond his physical strength to defeat him.

However, Giyu ducks and tries again, but this time, Akaza is struck in the neck and is bleeding. However, the bleeding was stopped immediately after striking because of his regeneration. Akaza realized that Giyu had unlocked his Demon Slayer Mark. Akaza then increased his punch strength and speed by just over ten and punched within a blink of an eye.

Giyu, with his Demon Slayer Mark, tries to attack Akaza.

Giyu uses his 4<sup>th</sup> Water Breathing technique to slice Akaza's right arm but notices that Akaza has already struck the other side of his head. Seeing this wide opening from Akaza's back, Tanjiro tries to attack with his Hinokami Kagura on Akaza's exposed neck. However, Akaza watched the blade without even seeing it. After that, Akaza continues to overwhelm Tanjiro and Giyu together.

Giyu has used all his Water Breathing techniques only to see that Akaza has adapted to all of his techniques. Akaza rushed forward to finally kill Giyu by appreciating him for fighting this long. Meanwhile, Tanjiro was awake and was trying to enter the Selfless State Giyu struck Akaza again to try to cut off his head. However, Akaza responded by dodging the blow and using the side of his fist to break Giyu's sword. Giyu then becomes stunned by having his sword broken, and Akaza farewells him by crouching down, preparing to strike right through Giyu's chest.

Akaza's hand was cut by Tanjiro in the middle of a fierce fight with Giyu & saving him from death.

However, right before touching Giyu's chest, Akaza's hand was severed by Tanjiro in an instant saving Giyu from Death. Tanjiro has now entered his Selfless State and was able to bypass Akaza's Compass Needle.

Tanjiro's appearance after entering the Selfless State

After entering the Selfless state, Akaza could not track the movements of Tanjiro as if he was standing & moving like a tree that should not exist in a battle. Akaza was dealing with something he had no experience with for over 160 years. Akaza & Giyu was confused by his speed & reflexes. Giyu then witnessed something unimaginable. Akaza was able to adapt to the speed within a few seconds. That is when Giyu realized why Akaza defeated Rengoku Kyojuro ( The Flame Hashira ).

The battle grew more and more intense between Akaza, Giyu, and Tanjiro. However, Tanjiro was punched by Akaza so hard that he crashed through 3 walls. By watching this, Giyu was sure that even with his Demon Slayer Mark awakened, he was still weak to defeat Akaza. Akaza then announces to Giyu, "Do not die like Kyojuro and Tanjiro," after assuming that Tanjiro has died from his punch. However, Tanjiro suddenly appeared behind Akaza unnoticed. Giyu was confident that he would cut Akaza's neck without his awareness. Nevertheless, Tanjiro screamed out Akaza's name and rushed toward him to attack him.

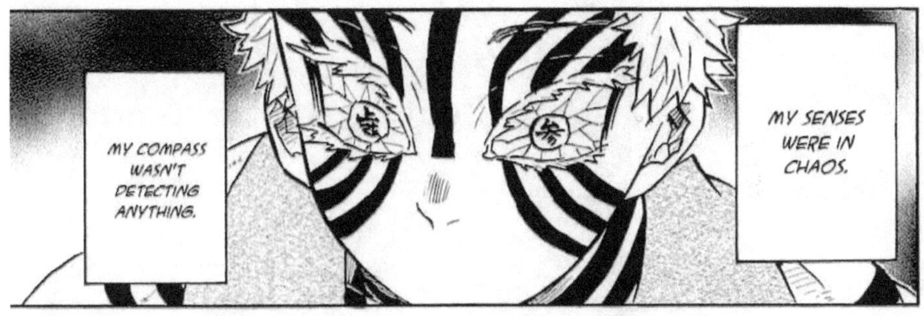

Akaza realizes that Tanjiro's battle spirit is gone, and he cannot even detect it with his compass.

Akaza then realized that Tanjiro was not dead and that his battle spirit was gone again, and this time it was at such a level that it was like he was not even alive. Akaza then tries to calm himself down, thinking he will be able to sense an attack presence. However, Tanjiro sliced off his head using the Hinokami Kagura Setting Sun technique. Tanjiro's this transformation left Giyu in total shock, while Akaza is still trying to understand what happened as he tries to put his head back with the resolve that he can still fight. However, Giyu throws his broken sword at Akaza's head, knocking it away from his gasp.

Akaza resolves that he can still fight while trying to attach his decapitated head.

When Akaza's body did not disintegrate, Giyu & Tanjiro started to worry. To their surprise, Akaza's headless body activated the destructive death compass needle again. He immediately tries to hit Tanjiro's neck but barely misses, knocking out Tanjiro unconscious. Giyu sees Akaza going for unconscious Tanjiro and uses Water Breathing to stop him. However, Akaza's body recovers instantly. Giyu screams, "If you want to kill Tanjiro, then you will have to kill me first." After this, Akaza realizes his indomitable spirit, which does not bend in the face of any obstacle.

Meanwhile, Giyu tries to learn Akaza's fighting pattern to fight again. He realizes the severity of the situation, he has reached his limit, and his body is starting to feel numb. He also realizes that breathing is the only thing keeping him alive. Nevertheless, Giyu focuses on protecting unconscious Tanjiro as he remembers his resolve not to let any family member or friends die on his watch again, knowing that Tanjiro would have done the same.

Suddenly Akaza stops his regeneration and remembers his past, where he sees his father, wife & Kaizo family. Finally, he decides that he does not want to fight anymore and gives up. Tanjiro, after regaining consciousness, and Giyu watch Akaza's body eventually fades into ash. A Kasugai Crow calls out after the battle and tells everyone that Tanjiro and Giyu have defeated Upper Moon 3 but are now unconscious. After some time, the duo regains consciousness and attempts to find the other Demon Slayers.

Muzan, in his final form.

While running through the hallway, they witness that Muzan ( In his original form ) has appeared right in front of them. Muzan then tells how persistent they were, which sickens him to the bottom of his every heart ( Remember that Muzan has seven hearts and five brains ). Muzan also says Demon Slayers always discuss avenging their families and friends. He also says they should be thankful for not dying and continue living.

Muzan suddenly attacks the Demon Slayers, and they can barely dodge the attack. Muzan unleashes an even more powerful attack, which Giyu barely blocks with his Dead Calm technique. Tanjiro cannot keep up with his attacks and dodges them on instinct but still attempts to close the distance. However, before he can attack him, Muzan manages to cut Tanjiro's right eye. Giyu then quickly saves Tanjiro and warns him not to get too close.

Muzan suddenly attacks Tanjiro and Giyu.

He also says the sun does not penetrate the Infinity castle. Muzan asks if three Hashiras are enough to kill him, and this word surprises Tanjiro and Giyu while Muzan continues to attack them. He also says that his subordinates have already killed Obanai ( The Serpent Hashira ) and Mitsuri ( The Love Hashira ). He says he has seen this by Nakime (Upper Moon 4) 's eye. Suddenly to Muzan's surprise, he gets ambushed by Mitsuri and Obanai together, who are alive.

Mitsuri and Obanai ambush Muzan.

After seeing this, Muzan gets confused and wonders how the two Hashiras he had seen dead are still alive. He angrily yells Nakime's name and asks her what is going on. Meanwhile, Yoshiro ( The good Demon & former partner of Tamayo ) responds to him, saying that he is now in control of Infinity Castle.

Yoshiro manipulates Nakime's vision.

Muzan suddenly changes his attention to the battlefield as Giyu and Obanai attack him with their breathing Styles. Muzan realizes he will not be able to fight the Hashiras and Yoshiro. So he clenches his fist and destroys Nakime's skull, which crushes the Infinity Castle, leaving them in the streets.

Muzan then comes out of the rubble while throwing the blocks in every direction. Enraged, he yells at the Demon Slayers and says he will kill every one of them before Sunrise. Giyu, Obanai, and Mitsuri attack Muzan to engage him in battle; however, they all get hit as Muzan unleashes another flurry of attacks. He commends them for being able to move and acknowledges that those with Demon Slayer Marks will not fail quickly.

As the battle continues, Giyu becomes weak due to the poison Muzan inflicted during his attack. His sword also gets taken away by one of Muzan's whips. Sanemi then intervenes while grabbing his sword and throwing it near Giyu and yells that he should be focused or get killed. Giyu then holds the blade's word and attacks Muzan with Water Breathing as he thinks he will not look back again and will keep fighting till the end.

Muzan then admits they are more resilient than expected but is also unconcerned as it is only a matter of time before his poison kills them all, long before Sunrise. Suddenly Tamayo's cat jumps into the fight and injects him with an antidote that will eventually turn him into a human. Obanai then manages to awaken his Demon Slayer Mark and turns his sword red. He then slices off Muzan's arm, which causes Muzan to stop for a second. Seeing this, Sanemi yells at Giyu and tells him to get prepared as he charges toward Giyu, and they both attack each other's swords, turning them red.

Suddenly out of nowhere, Muzan attacks with his special attack, which knocks all Demon Slayers unconscious. However, Tanjiro manages to avoid the attack as he rages toward Muzan. After a long battle between Tanjiro and Muzan, Tanjiro, with the help of an open eye, manages to pin down Muzan against the wall resolving that he will keep him pinned down until Sunrise but fails as his left arm gets chopped off by Muzan's attack.

Tanjiro tries to pin down Muzan.

Afterward, Giyu appears behind him and pushes the sword with Tanjiro to pin Muzan down. Now with both Demon Slayers holding Muzan down with their blade and strength combined, the edges turn red, resulting in Muzan coughing off blood from his mouth. Soon the sun starts to rise slowly & Muzan thinks of a way to get out of there. As he began to disintegrate, he started to cover himself by growing fat outer flesh around his body that looked like a giant demon baby to block the sunlight from entering/ touching his main body.

As the flesh grew outwards, it also began to pull Tanjiro inside of it. Tanjiro then gives Giyu a brutal headbutt from letting him get sucked along with him, and he then gets swallowed along with his sword. Giyu tries hard to yell out Tanjiro's name.

Muzan is in his giant from a baby while Giyu tries to pull out Tanjiro.

Meanwhile, Muzan tries to dig a massive hole in the ground to save himself from the sun while Giyu and Sanemi attack him with their Breathing Styles to prevent him from escaping. Sanemi also joined them and unleashed his attack. Tanjiro then attacks Muzan from inside, causing him to scream in agony before disintegrating once and for all.

After the fight, Giyu tries to find Tanjiro and sees him kneeling while still holding his sword. The Kakushi team then informs Giyu that Tanjiro is no longer breathing & his pulse is also gone. Giyu then started crying and kneeled before Tanjiro. Furthermore, he grabbed Tanjiro's hand, apologized for failing to protect him, and said he was the one who ended up receiving protection from Tanjiro.

Tanjiro kneeled with no breathing and pulse after the fight.

Note from Author: What happens after this fight will be told in later books. There are more Hashiras whose stories are yet to be told.

www.ingramcontent.com/pod-product-compliance
Lightning Source LLC
Chambersburg PA
CBHW021143130726
47988CB00003B/1438